BREWSTER'S COURAGE

Debrah Kovac

BREWSTER'S COURAGE

WRITTEN BY
DEBORAH KOVACS

ILLUSTRATED BY
JOE MATHIEU

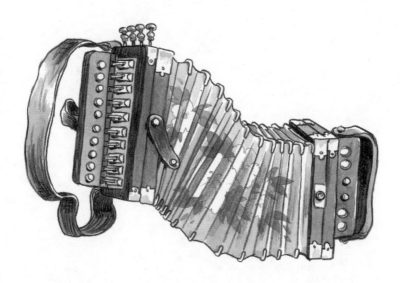

SIMON & SCHUSTER BOOKS FOR YOUNG READERS
Published by Simon & Schuster
New York   London   Toronto   Sydney   Tokyo   Singapore

For Jim

SIMON & SCHUSTER BOOKS FOR YOUNG READERS
Simon & Schuster Building, Rockefeller Center
1230 Avenue of the Americas, New York, New York 10020
Text copyright © 1992 by Deborah Kovacs
Illustrations copyright © 1992 by Joe Mathieu
All rights reserved including the right of reproduction
in whole or in part in any form.
SIMON & SCHUSTER BOOKS FOR YOUNG READERS
is a trademark of Simon & Schuster.
Designed by Vicki Kalajian
The text of this book is set in 13 pt. Goudy Old Style.
The illustrations were done in pencil and wash.
The display type is Announcement Roman.
Manufactured in the United States of America

10 9 8 7 6 5 4 3 2 1

Library of Congress Cataloging-in-Publication Data
Kovacs, Deborah. Brewster's courage / by Deborah Kovacs ; pictures
by Joe Mathieu. p. cm. Summary: Enchanted by the music of Wild Turkey
and the Loblollies, Brewster Ferret follows them to their home
in a Louisiana bayou and tries to make a place for himself
in the animal community there. [1. Ferret—Fiction.
2. Animals—Fiction. 3. Bayous—Fiction. 4. Louisiana—Fiction.
5. Musicians—Fiction.] I. Mathieu, Joseph, ill. II. Title.
PZ7.K8565Br 1992 [Fic]—dc20 91-21481 CIP
ISBN: 0-671-74016-4

CONTENTS

Acknowledgments:

Thanks to Queen Ida, also known as Ida Guillory, leader
of Queen Ida and her Bon Temps Zydeco Band, for her
encouragement, and for her suggestions on the lyrics to Wild
Turkey's songs. Thanks to the members of the band Magnolia for
reviewing the descriptions of the look and sound of traditional
Cajun musical instruments. Finally, thanks to all the Cajun and
Zydeco musicians who supplied the inspiration for this book.
We hope you like it.

Note: Wild Turkey's songs are written in "Cajun patois,"
the form of French spoken in the Bayou regions of Louisiana.

"Be what you is."

—Clifton Chenier
The King of Zydeco

1

IN WHICH WE MEET BREWSTER
AND HE DISCOVERS HIS LOVE OF MUSIC

Brewster was a black-footed ferret, born in a dark tunnel somewhere beneath the South Dakota prairie. More than anything, he loved to ride his bicycle. It was a gift from his Uncle Rex, who said, "Someday you'll long to see the world. I hope you'll ride this bicycle to an adventure so exciting, you can't even imagine it."

Now, Uncle Rex had never been out of South Dakota himself. In fact, he only rarely left the tunnels his family had dug for generations. But he had a mind filled with dreams, and his nephew did, too.

Day after day, Brewster rode his bicycle, leaving the burrow at sunrise and returning at sunset, searching for his great adventure. He traveled in every possible direction, finding nothing remarkable. He rode until he thought he had seen everything there was to see in the world. Of course, all he had seen was a stretch of South Dakota. But he didn't know that—not yet.

One fine morning, his life changed forever. He rode to a huge bronze statue of a buffalo. Tourists often swarmed over the statue.

That day, Brewster was alone. He scrambled onto the statue's back and caught his breath. (He had been riding hard for some time.) He sniffed the breeze. "New-mown hay. My favorite smell," he said, stretching his stiff limbs in the warm sunshine. He shaded his eyes and scanned the dusty red prairie, bare but for clumps of trees on the horizon. A moving shape  caught his eye. He sat bolt upright. "What's *that?*" he wondered.

He saw a big, rusty, dusty bus. It headed straight for the statue, but screeched to a halt just in time. A hand-painted sign on its side read Here Comes Wild Turkey and the Loblollies from the Moustafaya Swamp in the Louisiana Bayou Country.

Brewster stared at the curious sign, whispering the odd words to himself. Then the bus door flew open. He blinked and said, "What the . . ." Out stepped a turkey with bright red wattles and a puffy body, covered with brown, black, and white feathers. Right behind the turkey came a ring-tailed raccoon, handsome with black-masked eyes. Then a beaver with shabby, shaggy brown fur waddled out. A big old alligator with a shiny green hide crawled and bumped down the bus steps last. (He was too tall to fit through the bus door on his hind legs.) Brewster had never seen such strange-looking creatures before. They didn't notice him, way up on top of the buffalo statue, so he stared at them with great interest.

The turkey stretched his wings, then waggled each of his legs. "What a ri-i-i-de!" he hollered in a booming baritone. "Puts me in the mood for some *music!*"

"Suits me," called the beaver in a husky twang, flapping his flat tail.

"Let's play," squeaked the raccoon, clapping clappety-clap.

"Why wait?" roared the alligator. His teeth gnashed and gleamed.

"Music," whispered Brewster, leaning forward. Except for the moaning of the prairie wind on a cold winter night and some campfire songs his Uncle Rex had taught him, Brewster had never heard music before.

The turkey opened a crammed compartment in the bottom of the bus. The raccoon took out a fiddle and drew a bow across it: *ai-eee.* The alligator collected a curved, furrowed piece of metal and hung it over his shoulders. He ran his claws up and down the metal: *zing-zing.* The beaver slung a guitar over his shoulders and

strummed it: *chanh-chanh-ch-chanh*. The turkey pulled out a box with buttons on one side, a handle on the other, and folded-up fabric with a multicolored floral print in between. He tugged at both ends: *whin-hoo-la-la-de-de-de*.

The turkey shouted, "*Un! Deux! Trois!*" With an *ai-eee zing-zing chanh-chanh-ch-chanh whin-hoo-la-la-de-de-de*, Wild Turkey and the Loblollies made their music. They only played a few different notes; but driven by the rhythm of the alligator's *zings*, those notes spun and twirled, like a musical kaleidoscope that surprises you with every turn.

The sound was thrilling. Fur stood up in a straight line along Brewster's spine. He nearly swooned. "Music!" he breathed. He was so excited, he almost fell off his perch. He squeezed the buffalo statue tightly with his legs.

The turkey threw back his head and howled, "*Yay yiiiiii!*" He sang a long, lovely song in a language Brewster didn't understand. The turkey's voice was filled with sorrow and delight. When he sounded happy, Brewster's spirits soared. When he sounded sad, Brewster's heart melted. Chills passed through every inch of the ferret's body, starting at his whiskers and ending at the tip of his tail. "Am I dreaming?" he wondered.

Too soon, the musicians stopped playing. "Well, now, let's have a look at this here buffalo before we continue our national tour," said the turkey. He gazed respectfully at the big hunk of bronze. Then he noticed Brewster way up on top. Brewster looked back at him, afraid to breathe. "Hello there, little feller," said the turkey kindly. "Are you from around here?"

Brewster had to swallow a couple of times before he could

answer. "Yes, sir," he said finally, adding, "Your music is wonderful. I've never heard anything like it before."

"Thank you, thank you," said the turkey proudly. "If you ever get down to the Moustafaya Swamp in the Louisiana Bayou Country, come over and hear us. We play every Thursday night at the Jolie Blonde Café."

"I'll be there," said Brewster. At that moment, he knew his great adventure had begun.

"Well, we've got to hit the road," said the turkey to the other musicians. "We're due at the Corn Palace by nightfall," he explained to Brewster. "See you down on the bayou, little feller." Wild Turkey hopped back on the ramshackle bus, followed by the raccoon, beaver, and alligator. They all waved at Brewster.

Wild Turkey gunned the engine and backed out of the parking lot. As the bus drove away in a cloud of blue smoke, he tooted the horn three times. It sounded like a broken trombone.

Brewster shook his head. He couldn't believe what he had seen . . . or heard. But he knew that his days in South Dakota were numbered. "I wonder where the Louisiana Bayou Country is," he said as he pedaled back to the burrow.

That night, Brewster lay in the midst of his family, listening to them breathe and snuffle in their sleep. It was peaceful, but his eyes were wide open. He kept hearing the music of Wild Turkey and the Loblollies, and the haunting sounds of Wild Turkey's voice. And there was a wonderful place called Moustafaya Swamp, where he could hear them play every single Thursday night.

The next morning, his mind was made up. He shook the sleep off his fur and went to find his dear mother, who was in their big, cool storeroom, putting up food for the winter. "I'm leaving home now, Ma," he said, kissing her.

She glanced at him and nodded, her eyes sad. "I always knew this day would come," she said. "Where are you going?"

"To the Moustafaya Swamp in the Louisiana Bayou Country," said Brewster. He enjoyed saying those mysterious words out loud.

"That must be far away," said his mother, who didn't leave her burrow often. "You won't be able to visit our storeroom to get food. How will you keep yourself?"

"I expect I'll find work," said Brewster. "There must be some type of job for a healthy young ferret with a bicycle."

"We'll miss you, son," said his mother. "I'll wonder every night if you're fed, if you're warm, if you're safe. But the first time I saw you ride your bicycle, I knew that someday it would take you away from us." She hugged him. "We love you—the whole family. At least we can give you that."

"Thanks, Mom," said Brewster. He blinked back tears, and wondered if he should change his mind.

2

IN WHICH BREWSTER LEAVES HIS FAMILY AND JOURNEYS TO THE MOUSTAFAYA SWAMP

That very day, Brewster loaded his few belongings into his saddlebags. His family gathered to say good-bye. He hugged each of them and said, "Don't worry about me. I'll always land on my feet."

Uncle Rex was wistful. He said, "Good luck, son. Kind of wish I was going with you myself." He pulled out a worn leather pouch and extracted an ancient five-dollar bill that had been folded and refolded many times. "I always kept this aside in case I ever decided to hit the road," he said. "Doesn't look to me like that's ever going to happen. It'd make me proud to know that you were using it."

"Thanks, Uncle Rex," said Brewster, gripping the money gratefully before tucking it into a zippered pocket. Tears welled up in his eyes. He turned his head to blink them away. When he turned back, he saw his whole family standing before him in a semicircle. He looked at each one of them for a long time, memorizing their dear faces. "I'll miss you all," he said, swallowing hard. Then he hopped on his bicycle and rode off.

The highways between South Dakota and Louisiana were big and busy. They weren't built for bicycles, either. So Brewster figured out a route that bypassed those speedways. Day melted into day, mile into mile, as Brewster pedaled steadily to his destination, stopping only to camp out at night. The highlight was a stay in Marshall, Missouri, where he sampled a stack of the most delicious flapjacks it was ever his pleasure to eat.

Each day, as he rode, Brewster enjoyed the new sights around him—the towns and cities, the farmland stretching out in each direction. But the nights were lonely. Brewster huddled next to his tiny campfire, eating a simple supper of canned beans or peas before crawling into his tent. At those moments, thoughts of home and family filled his mind. More than once, he would wonder, "Am I doing the right thing?" But then he would remember the beautiful music of Wild Turkey and the Loblollies, and his heart would fill with hope once again.

"Everything will be okay once I get to the Moustafaya Swamp," he whispered every night as he lay down to sleep. He spoke so firmly that he almost believed himself.

For fourteen days, Brewster traveled, weaving across the landscape by day, camping by the side of the road every night. Finally, he came to a sign that read Welcome to Bayou Country. "Hot dog!" Brewster shouted.

He was so happy, he hopped off his bicycle and danced a little jig. "I'm here! I'm here!"

"You sure aren't making a secret of *that* piece of news," growled a voice from behind a stump. "Can't a fellow get a little sleep around here?"

Brewster stopped his dance and tiptoed around to the back side of the stump. There was the biggest, fattest muskrat he had ever seen. The muskrat was so fat, he seemed about to bust out of his fur. The fat came down from his chin in rolls, in billows. He didn't breathe so much as he wheezed. He lay on his back, his head propped up on a log, his arms folded over his rippling belly. He eyed Brewster through two suspicious slits while picking his teeth with a bit of straw. "Well, lookit what just rolled into Bayou Country," the muskrat said. "Just what kind of animal do you pretend to be?"

"I'm a black-footed ferret," said Brewster, drawing himself proudly up to his full height. "My kind are very rare."

"Rare, are they?" giggled the muskrat. "Well, that's a blessing, at any rate."

Brewster wasn't sure if this cross old creature was friend or foe. But he did need some help, so he decided to take a chance. "Could you possibly direct me to the Moustafaya Swamp?" he asked.

The muskrat guffawed, creating a powerful gust of wind that almost knocked Brewster over backward. "Now, why would a creature so *rare* as yourself want to go to a forgotten, overlooked, raggedy old place like the Moustafaya Swamp?" the muskrat asked.

Brewster's eyes twinkled. Dreamily, he thought about the reason for his voyage. Surely the muskrat would understand. "I heard the music of Wild Turkey and the Loblollies. It changed my life! I left my home, my family, and the dusty South Dakota prairie. I have traveled fourteen days and camped out fourteen nights to move here to Bayou Country, so I can hear Wild Turkey and his band play every Thursday night at the Jolie Blonde Café."

The muskrat rumbled with laughter until every bit of fur on his body rolled and jiggled.

Brewster was taken aback. "What's so funny?" he asked.

"That's the gol-danged *silliest* reason I *ever* heard of for somebody to up and leave his home," the muskrat said, chuckling. "Imagine traveling for fourteen days and fourteen nights just to hear some of that old chanky-chank music. You must be out of your head! How long you planning to stay, anyway?" he asked, as though he figured the answer would be, "About fifteen minutes."

"I plan to live there forever," said Brewster, gazing into the distance as though he could see a picture of his own future. "I never want to be more than a few minutes away from the Jolie Blonde Café."

"And how are you planning to make a living, you skinny little thing?" asked the muskrat.

Brewster had puzzled about this several times as he headed down from South Dakota. He hadn't come up with a good idea, at least not yet. But he didn't want the muskrat to know that. What business was it of his, anyhow? So Brewster smiled brightly. He said, "I've got some prospects over there," though privately he wondered what the prospects might be.

The muskrat waved him away with a flap of his leathery paw. "Well, you seem to have your mind made up, all right. Don't suppose it would do me any good to hold off telling you how to get to the Moustafaya Swamp. It's about fifteen miles down the road. Turn right at the red brick house. But don't go inside. There's some wild boars live there that are mighty unfriendly. Now, get out of here and let me get some sleep!" With that, the muskrat heaved himself over onto one side. Soon, he was snoring loudly.

Back on his bicycle, Brewster pedaled south. He couldn't tell fifteen miles, but finally he saw the red brick house, just as the muskrat had described it. At the window, Brewster noticed a wild boar, his face pressed against the glass so tightly that steam had

formed around his nostrils. In the bright sunshine, Brewster could just make out the boar's yellow eyes and the curl of his sharp tusks. To be safe, Brewster veered his bicycle over to the other side of the road, pedaling at top speed.

Just after the boars' house, Brewster saw a sign that read Moustafaya Trail. A big arrow pointed west. Brewster's heart thumped. "Almost there!" he shouted. "I can't believe it!" He was so happy, he stood up in the saddle to pick up speed, then followed the arrow.

The landscape on either side of the trail grew sodden. Thick stands of trees soaked in brackish water. Fuzzy clumps of Spanish moss hung from every treetop, almost to the surface of the murky bayou water. Birds called languidly, bullfrogs twanged. The air was hot and heavy.

As he rode farther along the trail, Brewster grew weary. Here, the trees met overhead, forming a canopy. It was like riding through a tunnel. Soon night would fall. Now the frogs and birds started to sound different to Brewster . . . a little bit creepy. Maybe he should find a place to camp for the night. But where? The swamp was not welcoming. Homesickness ran through Brewster as sharp as a fever. He took a deep, shaky breath. "What am I doing here?"

He couldn't guess how far it would be before he met anybody, so he decided to return to the crossroads and camp there for the night. "I'll try again in the morning," he thought, and pedaled back to the red brick house. Across the road was a stand of cedar trees. Though the trees had a strong, unpleasant odor and their branches were scratchy, there, at least, Brewster felt protected enough to set up camp for the night.

He was too unsettled to cook dinner, so he got ready for bed instead. Then he peeked at the red brick house across the road. Four pairs of yellow eyes stared back at him through a front window. Brewster shuddered. He scrambled into his tent and zipped it shut. He got into his sleeping bag and pulled it over his head, wondering if he would ever get to sleep.

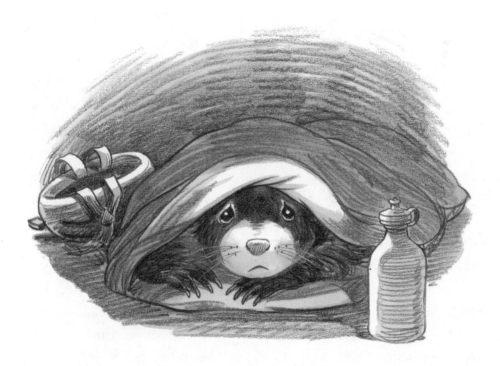

3

IN WHICH BREWSTER ARRIVES AT MOUSTAFAYA SWAMP AND MEETS A MOST HELPFUL ALLIGATOR

The next morning, Brewster crawled out of his tent. He sniffed the air for a sign of fresh water somewhere around so that he could freshen up a bit with a sponge bath, or maybe even a swim. But the slow, hot breezes that blew past carried no hint of water.

Brewster packed his tent, sleeping bag, and saddlebags, and rolled his bicycle out from under the cedars. The four boars sat on the steps of their red brick house. Their arms were folded across their chests. They didn't look friendly.

Brewster smiled, anyway, and hopped on his bicycle. As he rode past the boars, all four of them snapped their heads in his direction. They glared as he passed by. "Nice welcome," muttered Brewster. "Oh, well. Things are bound to get better."

This time, the trip along the trail didn't seem so long. Maybe it was the promise Brewster had made himself that he could have a whole can of green peas once he got to where he was going. Maybe it was the fresh morning air and the bright blue sky. Or maybe it was his optimistic heart, which never allowed him to lose hope.

Brewster reached a clearing in the swamp. There was a rickety dock with a sign that read Wait Here for Swamp Sallie's Bayou Tours. Next Tour: 9 o'clock.

Brewster had never worn a wristwatch. He glanced at the sky. According to the sun, it was almost nine o'clock. "I guess I'm somewhere," he thought. He got off his bicycle and dug into the can of peas. He had just polished them off, and had paused to splash a little swamp water on his face, when he heard a motor's chug in the distance. "I wonder if this could be Swamp Sallie?" he said to himself. He rushed to the edge of the broken-down dock and peered toward the sound.

He saw a squat, wide-beamed, slow-moving aluminum boat. Seated in the stern was perhaps the largest and oldest lady alligator in the world. She wore a bright red sundress, a huge, floppy straw hat, and a grin as big as her head. When she saw Brewster standing on the end of the dock, her grin stretched even wider. "Hello, son!" she called in a husky baritone. The alligator reached over with her stubby arms and turned off the boat's engine. She glided up on the dock. "You weren't looking to go on a tour of the bayou by any chance, were you?" she asked.

Brewster was happy to hear friendly words. "Would you be willing to show me around?" In spite of his best effort, his voice wobbled. He hoped she wouldn't notice.

"Well, now," she said, as she cocked her head and looked at him. "Just what type of animal are you, anyway? I don't think I've ever seen your kind in these parts."

Brewster hesitated just long enough to swallow his fear. "I'm a traveling ferret," he explained. "I'm out to see the world."

"Is that how you got to this back-of-beyond pocket?" the alligator asked cheerfully.

"Well, yes," began Brewster, leaping at the chance to explain himself to somebody who was willing to listen. In a rush, he

said, "Iamablack-footedferret, averyrarecreature.Ileftmyhome inSouthDakota fifteendaysagobecauseofmygreatdesiretolivehere inthisswamp,soIcangohearWildTurkeyandtheLoblolliesplay everyThursdaynightattheJolieBlondeCafé."

The alligator grinned even wider. "Let me show you around your new home!" she boomed. "Hop aboard!" Brewster glanced at his bicycle and other belongings. The alligator said, "Bring those things along, too. There's plenty of room." So Brewster lifted everything aboard, and the alligator pulled the starter cable on her engine. The engine coughed once or twice, and then it caught.

"That engine's never failed me yet, but sometimes it makes like it will," she chortled. "By the way, the name's Swamp Sallie," she said. "What's yours?"

"I'm Brewster—Brewster Ferret," was the reply.

"I like that name," mused Swamp Sallie. "It sounds honest."

"Gee, thanks," said Brewster. He felt shy and dipped his head. It was too exciting to meet somebody called Swamp Sallie.

"Now, what type of tour do you want today?" asked Swamp Sallie, steering her little craft to the middle of the swamp waters. "Shall I do my 'Tourist Just Passing Through Without a Deep Interest in Learning About the Moustafaya Swamp' tour? Or do you want the deluxe tour? That's the one I call 'I'm Here Now, I'm Here Forever, and I Want to See My New Home.'"

"I like the sound of that one," said Brewster. "But I'm not sure I can afford it."

Swamp Sallie looked him up and down. "I'll take an I O U," she said. "When you get on your feet, you can do me a favor sometime. Now, set back and enjoy the ride." She gunned her engine to its maximum speed of about two knots per hour—about as fast as Brewster would get along on land if he crawled on his belly through quicksand.

As they traveled, Brewster stared at the dense growth on the banks of the swamp. Everything looked so unfamiliar. On the prairie, he could see for miles in every direction. Here, the trees grew close together on the shore, their roots poking up through the mud at the water's edge. Heavy vines trailed from branch to branch. Clumps of plants with round leaves and lavender-colored flowers floated in the brown water.

Swamp Sallie sputtered, "Blast those foolish nutrias! Here they come!"

Brewster peered into the water, not knowing what to expect. He didn't see anything. "What? Where?" he said.

"There! And there!" said Swamp Sallie, pointing impatiently. Brewster squinted at the water again. Then he saw what Swamp Sallie was talking about. Swimming quickly in their direction were ten furry animals with little beady eyes and biggish, bewhiskered noses. "If those creatures aren't the silliest living things on earth, I'll eat my hat," muttered Swamp Sallie.

Brewster eyed Swamp Sallie's sharp yellow teeth and wondered what she did eat. But he decided not to ask.

The nutrias' heads shot out of the water. They were sleek, furry, and fat. Their beady eyes looked empty of thoughts or ideas. They stared at Swamp Sallie and at Brewster. Then they disappeared under the water and paddled away.

"What's wrong with them?" asked Brewster.

"Nothing, I suppose," growled Swamp Sallie. "Except they

just take up space. They don't add anything to this world. They nibble through the riverbanks, too. They made one of my favorite cyprus trees fall over just the other day. And every time I turn around, it seems like there are more of them."

Since there weren't many black-footed ferrets around, especially in the Moustafaya Swamp, Brewster reasoned that this was a complaint Swamp Sallie was not likely to voice about him. Still, he wondered if she might think that *he* was a creature who just took up space, too. But one quick glance at her friendly face relieved him of that worry.

The little boat chugged around a bend in the swamp. There, at the base of a big tree, was a little shack with a sign on top that read Jolie Blonde Café. "That's it!" squeaked Brewster, jumping up and pointing. The boat swayed.

"Sit down or you'll fall into the swamp," said Swamp Sallie, chuckling. "That's the place, all right. It's humble, I suppose. But they sure do make good music there on Thursday nights. Hey! That's tonight!"

"It's Thursday?" said Brewster, his eyes widening and his heart beating faster. "Oh, boy! And here I am! I can't believe it!" Hold-

ing on to his seat, he rocked back and forth and imagined the
music he would hear that night.

"You should head there around sunset," advised Swamp Sallie.
"That way, you'll get the best seat. That is, if the wild boars don't
edge you out."

Brewster shivered. He imagined the boars shoving him out of
the way, or worse, sitting right on top of him.

"I guess you've already run into them," said Swamp Sallie.
"Well, don't pay them any mind. They look mean, but they won't
hurt you any."

The little boat chugged past another cabin on the swamp edge.
"That's the Moustafaya Store," said Swamp Sallie. "It's run by a
family of raccoons. It's got most of what you need. There's a post
office in there, too. But don't use it. Those raccoons read everybody's mail, and they'll tell the whole swamp your secrets." She
shook her head. Then, spotting a raccoon on the porch, she
roared, "Hello there, Hector! Read any good postcards lately?"

"Why, Sallie!" said the raccoon, embarrassed. Then he
noticed Brewster. The raccoon stared at the ferret, taking him in,
then scurried back into the store.

Swamp Sallie sent up a chuckle. "Oh, he's such an old gossip,"
she whispered to Brewster. "And the worst of it is, he just won't
admit it! But don't mind him. Don't mind anybody around here.
They're just set in their ways. They're not used to seeing outsiders. And it takes a long time for an outsider to become an insider.
I guess folks want to make sure you're really going to stick around
before they take the trouble to get to know you."

Brewster had never been an outsider before. He didn't like the

feeling. At least Swamp Sallie was nice to him. He smiled. "You're different, aren't you?"

"I suppose I am," Swamp Sallie agreed. "I've always been the curious type. That's kept me going—right here and in my travels around the world." Brewster looked surprised. Sallie said, "That's right, I've been a few places in my time. One day I'll show you my postcard collection. But right now, we're getting to my favorite part of the tour. Want to meet some of my relations?"

"Sure," said Brewster, leaning forward and looking around.

"Now, I got to warn you," said Swamp Sallie. "If you ran into my relations when you were by yourself, you'd find them to be the unfriendliest group of animals you ever saw. They'd make the wild boars look like the Welcome Wagon. But I visit them whenever I'm in this part of the swamp. After all, they're family. And I always bring them a little something special to eat." She opened a metal box at the bottom of the boat. Inside were about thirty pieces of fried chicken. Swamp Sallie picked up a sharpened stick and stabbed some of the chicken. Then she started to croon.

"He-e-e-e-e-e-e-re, baby," she called softly. "He-e-e-e-e-e-e-re, baby!"

Within a few minutes, the water surrounding the boat was crowded with the enormous muzzles of alligators, all snapping open and shut in search of Swamp Sallie's chicken. Their gaping

maws gave Brewster the willies. He trembled. "Don't you worry, sweetie," cooed Swamp Sallie. "They won't hurt you none. It's not their fault they have such big, hungry mouths. Just be sure to keep your whole body inside the boat. All right, sugar?"

Brewster made himself as small as possible. The alligators bumped the boat and rocked it from side to side as Sallie stabbed chicken part after chicken part. The alligators gnashed and smashed their teeth.

When all the chicken was gone, she called out, "That's all, cousins."

They opened their mouths and gurgled, "Thanks, Sallie." Then they slipped away beneath the surface of the waters.

"They love my fried chicken," Sallie said, beaming. She started the engine once again, and the tour continued. After a while, she asked, "How do you plan to earn your living in these parts?"

Stumped by this question for the second time in two days, Brewster didn't answer at first. Then he sighed, admitting, "I don't know."

"Thought so," said Sallie crisply. "Well, you've got to do something, don't you?" she said. "You can't go around eating tree bark. How much money do you have?"

"About three dollars," said Brewster. "*And* four cans of peas."

"That won't hold you for too long," said Sallie. "Those raccoons charge the earth and the stars for every single thing in that silly store. You've got to get to where you grow your own food. Then you'll be okay. But until then, you've got to earn your money somehow. . . . *Hmmm.*" She tapped her jaw for a few minutes, pondering this problem. Then her eyes lit on Brewster's bicycle. "That's it!" she said.

"What?" said Brewster, looking around.

"You can be a bicycle messenger!" proclaimed Sallie.

"What on earth is that?" asked Brewster.

"I found out about bicycle messengers when I was touring the sewers of New York City," said Sallie. "They pedal all over the place, carrying letters, packages, and what-have-you. The animals around here are so lazy, I bet they'd love to have somebody fetch and tote for them. What do you think?"

"I'll take the job!" said Brewster, eager to begin at once.

"Now, not so fast," said Swamp Sallie. "This is just a little idea. *You've* got to make it happen. None of these animals is going to be any too eager to hire you. They'll treat you like dirt. Some of them may even cheat you out of your fees—if they hire you in the first place. But I suppose it's worth a try. You've got to do *something* if you want to stay around here. You won't make it on three dollars, that's for sure."

"And four cans of peas," Brewster pointed out.

"Right, dear," said Swamp Sallie gently. "Now, where do you want to live?"

"I don't know," said Brewster. "I just thought I'd pitch my tent somewhere. It doesn't much matter to me."

"I think I know just the spot," said Swamp Sallie. "You can live right next to my south dock. That way, we'll get to say hello to each other a couple of times a day."

Brewster liked the idea of living within sight of his new friend. "Where is it?" he asked.

"Right along here," she said, shutting off her engine and pulling up to another teetery dock. It was shaded by a large cypress tree. "You could sleep right under that tree," said Swamp Sallie. "And this is a pretty friendly place—for the Moustafaya area, I mean. Best of all, there's a dirt road that leads right from here to the Jolie Blonde Café."

"That's all I need to know!" said Brewster, scrambling out of the boat. He liked the shadiness, and he liked the location. "This looks fine," he said.

"I'll be on my way then," said Swamp Sallie, turning to start her engine.

"Will you be at the Jolie Blonde Café tonight?" asked Brewster.

"Nope, I've got a date with a beau down in Beaux Bridge this evening," said Swamp Sallie. "We're going to a little bistro down by the Mississippi for crawfish étoufeé." She licked her chops. "I'll see you around, though," she said, waving.

"Thanks for everything," called Brewster, as his only friend in Louisiana chugged away.

"Any time, neighbor," Sallie hollered. "Just keep working on that messenger business."

4

IN WHICH BREWSTER MAKES HIS CAMPSITE
AND VISITS THE JOLIE BLONDE CAFÉ

The sounds in the swamp around Brewster's campsite were unfamiliar. As he pulled out his tent and looked for a place to pitch it, he heard animals calling to each other: *hoo-hoo-hoo, rack-ee rack-ee, pata pata pata, chub chub chub.* Insects hummed: *thrum thrum thrumma thrumm.* Mosquito hawks swooped to the surface of the swamp water, with wings that zizzed so loudly they set Brewster's teeth on edge. He tried to spot the creatures that made these sounds, but all he could see were leaves, branches, and moss.

Brewster turned in a circle twice, looking for somewhere to pitch his tent. Then he found the spot. It was under a willow tree. The long, sweeping branches dipped to the ground to make a leafy green hideaway. Brewster walked beneath the willow's arching branches and called, "I'm home!"

His call startled blackbirds perched in the tree. They flew to the sky, squawking. "Sorry," said Brewster, embarrassed.

Brewster pitched the little blue tent with its opening facing the water, so he could see Swamp Sallie every time she went past. He

smoothed a patch of dirt and
then collected some stones,
which he put in a circle for
a fireplace.

Brewster drank from his
water bottle. It was almost
empty. "I'll have to find
some water," he said aloud,
sniffing the air. Peering
into the soupy swamp, he shook his head. "That's not it," he said.
"I need a spring."

"A spring?" said a voice behind him. "Where do you think
you'll find a spring?"

Brewster wheeled around. He saw a large bird with a long beak.
Beneath the beak, a soft pouch wiggled when the bird spoke. "I
beg your pardon?" said Brewster.

"I said, where do you think you'll find a spring around here?"
repeated the bird, as though he knew the answer to that and any
other question but didn't choose to share what he knew. Never-
theless, he extended a wing toward Brewster. "Name's Tompkin," he said. "I'm a pelican, you know. All my people have been
pelicans since time began."

"How do you do?" said Brewster. "I'm Brewster Ferret. I'm new
in these parts."

"Yes, I see," said the pelican, spreading his wings and lifting off
the ground. "Good luck finding water," he called over his shoulder as he flapped away.

"Hmmm . . . *he* wasn't much help," said Brewster. "But I'm

sure to find water around here somewhere." He opened a can of peas and sat on the dock to eat them. "Now, let's see. What should I do first to get my messenger business going?"

The sound of a splash drew Brewster's attention. A cluster of sleek, furry creatures swam by. They were about the same size as the nutrias. But the nutrias had blank faces with no expression. These animals were fun and full of life. They slapped each other, dove deep in the water, swam all over, and whooped it up. With a homesick pang, Brewster realized that they reminded him of his brothers and sisters. "Hey, you guys!" he called. "Do you mind if I join in?"

The creatures hadn't noticed Brewster at first. But once they did, they stopped stock-still and stared at him. One spoke. "Well, now," he said slowly. "And just who might *you* be?"

"I'm Brewster Ferret," said Brewster. "I'm new in these parts."

The creature who had been speaking was nudged by another, smaller one. "Harmie, we know all about him," said the smaller creature. "He's that new animal Hector Raccoon told us about. He's here to listen to Wild Turkey and the Loblollies. Came all the way from Alaska or someplace."

"South Dakota, actually," said Brewster. "Say, what type of animals are you?"

"For heaven's sake, Ferret, we're river otters," said one of them. She turned her back to Brewster and added, "Can you imagine somebody traveling all the way from the North Pole just to hear Wild Turkey play the accordion?" The river otters chuckled, a little nastily, and started to swim away. As they passed Brewster, they made sure to give him a good splash in the face.

"Nice meeting you," whispered Brewster, wiping away droplets of water, mingled with a few tears.

Brewster was so hurt by the way most of the animals at Moustafaya Swamp had greeted him, he thought about staying in his tent that evening. But when night fell, he knew there was no way he could be this close to his idols without hearing them play.

Still feeling sad, he got on his bike and switched on the headlight. He started riding to the Jolie Blonde Café, mumbling, "I hope nobody else is mean to me. I just can't figure it. If some animal came into our colony in South Dakota, we'd treat him like an honored guest. How come these animals here treat me as if I'm the worst guy in the world?"

"*Hiss!*" he heard.

"*Whoa!*" said Brewster, almost falling off his bicycle.

"*Watch where you're riding!*" said a reedy voice.

"I'm sorry," said Brewster, rattled. "I didn't mean any harm." He looked around to see who had hissed. At first, he saw nothing in the gathering gloom. Then he saw a dark green snake with a black-patterned back. The snake stuck out a small, forked tongue and waggled it at Brewster. The inside of its mouth was white.

"I'm *really* sorry," said Brewster, taken aback. There were no snakes like this where he came from, and he wasn't sure whether this one was friendly or not. From the looks of things, she wasn't.

"That's better, buster," said the snake huffily. "You know, if you're going to go around riding on a big, shiny, dangerous thing like *that*" — she darted out to touch Brewster's bicycle with her evil-looking forked tongue — "you should watch where you're going. You don't want to squish one of your new neighbors flat as a pancake."

"I never meant any harm," said Brewster.

"Oh, I'll get over it," said the snake, her humor starting to improve. "Where are you riding to in the dark of night, anyway?"

"I'm going to the Jolie Blonde Café," said Brewster.

"Is it Thursday night already?" said the snake, friendlier still. "Where does the time go? May I ride with you?"

Brewster was surprised that this snake wanted to spend time with him. "Might as well be nice to somebody who's being nice," he thought. So he said, "Sure! Hop aboard!"

The snake slithered up Brewster's front tire until she came to his handlebars. She twisted like a corkscrew until she had a good, tight hold. She turned around to speak to him again. "My name is

Cottonmouth," said the snake. "You must be that ferret I've heard about."

"That's right," said Brewster, amazed that the creatures of Moustafaya all knew who he was after only one day.

"Good luck making a home around here," hissed the snake. "If you're bayou born and bred, you'll never find faster friends. But if you're a stranger, it can take more than a lifetime to feel as though you belong."

"I'm beginning to realize that," said Brewster.

Even though Brewster and Cottonmouth arrived at the Jolie Blonde Café on the early side, it was already jammed. Just as Swamp Sallie had predicted, the wild boars filled four tables all by themselves — right next to the stage and the front door.

When Brewster came in, the boars drew their top lips back over their pointy teeth — and they weren't smiling! But when they saw Cottonmouth perched on Brewster's shoulder, their drawn lips descended. Was it because these big brutes feared the bite of Cottonmouth's sharp fangs, or was it because they saw Brewster was now protected by a local? It was hard to tell. In any case, Brewster was happy to be there with Cottonmouth.

As they moved through the crowded café, Brewster recognized many of the other patrons. In one corner, he saw Hector and his family of raccoons. Hector sat bolt upright when he saw Brewster enter the room. When he saw Cottonmouth at Brewster's side, the raccoon leaned forward and gripped the edges of the table. Hector cupped a paw in front of his mouth and began to whisper to the other members of his family, who leaned over to catch his every word. From time to time, they looked at Brewster and Cottonmouth. Then they continued to whisper.

The river otters were there, too. They slouched, rather than sat, in their seats, taking up more than their fair share of room. They cast not-too-friendly glances at Brewster and Cottonmouth.

In the center of the room, Tompkin the pelican was seated with a lovely lady pelican at his side. He dipped his head politely when he saw the latest arrivals.

And taking up almost every other available seat in the place were the nutrias. Each of them sat straight-backed on a chair, staring directly ahead. Though their eyes were open, it was hard to tell if they were awake or asleep. "What *is* it about those guys?" wondered Brewster.

"We've got to get those good-for-nothing river otters to move over so we can get a seat," hissed Cottonmouth in Brewster's ear.

"How are we going to do that?" said Brewster.

"I'll take care of it," said Cottonmouth. "Just carry me over there."

Brewster and Cottonmouth approached the river otters. The otters glared. But their expressions changed when Cottonmouth reared up to her full height and stuck out her tongue menacingly.

"Uh, would you like a seat?" said one of the otters.

"Yes, thank you," said Brewster and Cottonmouth at the same time. The river otters edged over as far away as possible from Brewster and his new friend, and looked at them nervously from time to time.

"Well, that's enough drama for one day," whispered Cottonmouth. "Now, I hope we can just sit back and enjoy some music."

The lights in the Jolie Blonde Café were dimmed. Onto the stage came Jolie Blonde herself. She was a middle-aged, middle-sized egret who wore a feather boa and a large slouch hat festooned with colorful scarves. She wore fancy jewelry that sparkled in the spotlights. "*Bon soir, bon soir, ma famille,*" she cooed into the microphone. "Welcome to another one of our little Thursday night parties, which we call *fais do-do*. Tonight I am happy to welcome our favorite musicians, just back from a whirl-

wind tour of the United States —
Wild Turkey and the Loblollies!

Tingles zinged up and down
Brewster's back. He clasped
his hands together in his lap
and sat forward. Tears came to
his eyes. He drew in his breath.
"I'm here," he whispered.
"I made it!"

Wild Turkey and the Loblollies swarmed onto the stage. The
group was larger than when Brewster had met them at the buffalo
memorial. They were now joined by an old, old turtle who
clapped a pair of spoons against his shell, a river otter who played
the bass viol, and a little mouse who played the harmonica while
two other mice held it.

For the first few minutes, the group warmed up the crowd.
They played with a heavy downbeat that passed through the
whole café, as everyone stamped his feet or slapped the table in
time to the music. The bass viol thrummed, the washboard
zinged, spoons clattered, and the little mouse blew the harmonica with all her heart.

Wild Turkey, his eyes closed as if he were in a trance, swayed
and played his accordion like there was no yesterday or tomorrow. He played *hee hee hee hawwnnh hawwnnh hawwnnh UHH
. . . hee hee hee hawwnnh hawwnnh hawwnnh UHH!* He was calm,
but the crowd was going wild. Everyone was waiting for him to
sing. He drew in his breath.

"AI—EEEEE," he howled, tucking into his first song as the

crowd cheered, whooped, and hollered. It was a spirited tune with a mournful twist. He sang:

> Ma 'teet fille, ma chère 'teet monde,
> Je t'aime, je t'aime pour toute ma vie.
> Je chante à toi, ma chère 'teet monde,
> Quitte-moi, quitte moi jamais.

Cottonmouth whispered to Brewster, "The song means, 'My little girl, my dear little world, I love you, I love you for my whole life. I sing to you, my dear little world, Don't leave me, don't ever leave me.'"

"Thanks," breathed Brewster. Hearing Wild Turkey sing again was worth everything he had been through, and more besides. The music was so beautiful, it sounded as if it came from the sky.

"I'll never leave this place," he whispered. "Everything will work out fine. I just know it!"

5

IN WHICH BREWSTER HAS A DREAM,
TRIES TO START HIS BUSINESS,
AND FEELS PAIN

Brewster lay in his tent that night, singing Wild Turkey's songs. When at last he grew drowsy, the songs began to change a little as they ran through his mind, becoming mingled with the whispering of breezes rustling leaves, the distant hooting of owls, the calls of geese, the baying of hounds, and the twanging of bullfrogs. Brewster slept.

He dreamed that Wild Turkey and the band had come to his campsite to serenade him. "I made up a song just for you, little ferret," called Wild Turkey. "Come out now and hear it!"

In his dream, Brewster peeked out of the door of his tent. Wild Turkey handed him a big iron triangle and a stick to hit it with. "Bang this whenever you hear the words 'ma maison,'" said Wild Turkey.

"I will," said Brewster, mystified.

The band began to play.
The accordion sounded happy and
light. Each of the instruments
followed suit. Brewster held the
triangle, waiting for the moment
to clang it. Wild Turkey sang:

Ma maison, ma maison, où est ma maison?
Je cherche ma maison toute ma vie.
Ma maison, ma maison, je l'ai trouvé.
Ma maison est là, avec mes chansons.

Brewster banged away on his triangle as if he was ringing the
bell at a fire station. In his grip, the whole heavy triangle trembled. "What does that song mean?" whispered Brewster when
Wild Turkey finished playing.

"That song means, 'My home, my home, where is my home?
I've looked for my home for all my life. My home, my home, I've
found it. My home is there, with the songs.' Don't give up. This
will all work out!" And with that, Wild Turkey and his band
faded away.

In his sleep, Brewster rolled over and felt comfortable. He
enjoyed his first truly untroubled night since leaving South
Dakota.

In the morning, Brewster crept out of his tent and stretched tall, his arms reaching for the blue sky. "I'm gonna make it!" he shouted.

"Gonna make what?" hissed Cottonmouth, perched for a sunbath on a big, flat rock nearby.

"Today is the day I'm going to start the Moustafaya Bicycle Messenger Service," said Brewster. "It's going to work. I just know it will!"

"I'm glad to see you're so enthusiastic," said Cottonmouth, yawning. "I'm sure things will go your way." She didn't sound at all convinced.

Brewster opened a can of peas and ate them hurriedly. "I'm just going to ride around and tell everybody how I can help them," he said, speaking with confidence as he poked peas into his mouth. "I know I can help everyone here. They've got to believe me."

"I've got just one piece of advice for you," drawled Cottonmouth. "And I'm telling you this as a friend. Don't act too desperate. They'll see right through you. Do you get my meaning?"

"Not really," said Brewster. "How do I keep from acting desperate?"

"You've got to convince them that you've got something they need," said Cottonmouth. "You and I both know that none of these creatures is going to go one inch out of their way for you."

"I don't know how to be any other way than how I am," said Brewster, puzzled. "If that means that I'm going to seem desperate when I am desperate, well then, what can I do about it?"

"Every successful business has a good gimmick," said Cottonmouth. "Maybe you can think of one."

"Gimmick, gimmick," said Brewster. "Well, how about if I

promise to be faster than any other messenger they've ever used?"

"Try again, pal," said Cottonmouth. "They've never even heard of a messenger. They don't even know you exist. You know, I think you might need to do some advertising."

"Advertising?" said Brewster, befuddled. "I don't have enough money for another can of peas. How am I going to do any advertising?"

"Hector Raccoon runs a little radio station out of the back room of his store," said Cottonmouth. "Now, he's a lazy, good-for-nothing gossip, but he *does* have a little radio station. The station is only on the air for a few hours a week—on Friday mornings, as a matter of fact. Maybe you can convince him to put you on the radio for a few minutes." With that, Cottonmouth curled up on the rock, discontinuing conversation and continuing her sunbath.

"It's worth a try, I suppose," thought Brewster as he pedaled to Hector's store. When he got there, he found the whole raccoon clan rocking in chairs on the front porch. "Morning," he called, his voice wobbling only a little bit.

"Howdy," said Hector, bobbing his head a trace, his eyes narrowing a little as he looked Brewster up and down.

Before speaking again, Brewster collected his thoughts. "I've got to make it happen!" he whispered to the fluttery feeling of fear inside that was trying to trip him up. He stretched his face into the widest grin his mouth could make, cleared his throat, and said to Hector, "I have the *opportunity of a lifetime* for you today."

"Oh, yeah?" said Hector, pulling a nail file out of his vest pocket. He began to file his nails, looking mostly at them and, out of the corner of his eyes, a little at the trembling newcomer standing at the edge of the porch.

"I want to offer your radio station the *exclusive* opportunity to announce a new service that is available in this area for the very first time," said Brewster, smiling brightly.

"What sort of *service* is that?" said Hector, poorly concealing a bored yawn.

"Moustafaya Swamp is finally going to have something in common with New York City," said Brewster proudly.

"*What?*" said Hector, a rumble of laughter starting in his belly. "What on earth could we ever have in common with New York City?"

"Moustafaya Swamp now has its very own bicycle messenger service!" finished Brewster, forcing himself to ignore the sneer that was growing on Hector's face.

"And just what are we going to do with a bicycle messenger service?" said Hector.

"It'll be the fastest way of getting things around the swamp!" said Brewster. "Look. Say you have a customer all the way over on the other side of the swamp. Say that customer wants a pair of red socks. Say he's sick in bed, and he wants a pair of red socks—and right now. So he can't get to you to get the red socks, but with the Moustafaya Bicycle Messenger Service, you can get those socks to him the very same morning he wants them!" Brewster's eyes shone as he described his new service. He was sure he had the beginning of a great idea. But Hector's closed face showed him that he hadn't been convincing enough.

"We don't sell any red socks here," said Hector. "We only sell

blue socks. And all my customers come into the store. They *like* to come into the store. The store is the center of this swamp. I'm sorry, young fellow. You should take your New York City business idea somewhere else."

"Does this mean you won't give me a free ad on your radio show?" said Brewster, disheartened.

Hector's jaw dropped. "You must be joking!" he said, guffawing loudly. Beside him on the porch, his whole family joined in his laughter. "There is no way under the sun that I would give you *for free* even one minute of time on my radio station. Do you think I'm in business for my *health*? Go away, Ferret, go away. You're blocking my view." Hector sat back in his rocking chair, shaking his head in disbelief and chortling with his family.

Brewster climbed back on his bicycle, his head sunk low beneath his shoulders. "That didn't work very well," he murmured as he rode away. "I guess I acted too desperate." One tear, then another, slid from his eyes onto the bicycle handlebars. "Oh, Mother," he sighed, the tears falling faster now. "I miss you so much." He thought of his mother and his family, digging new tunnels, storing away food, curled up around each other like commas in the cozy security of the family burrow.

To calm himself, Brewster started to ride. He rode for a long, long time. He rode up and down the tiny towpaths that lined the Moustafaya Swamp. At some places, the pathway he rode on ended in a big, swampy puddle. When that happened, he would lift his bicycle over his head and slosh through the murky water until he reached dry land. Then he would hop back aboard and ride some more.

As he rode, the sun climbed high in the sky. When it sat dead overhead, a blistering ball that sent heat drumming down onto his back and neck, Brewster decided to rest for a bit. Just ahead he saw the river otters cavorting at a swimming hole. A thick vine dangled from an overhanging tree limb right into the center of a pool. The otters were swinging on the vine and dropping into the water. "That looks like fun," thought Brewster wistfully. But he didn't try to join them. He was sure he would be rejected. And

the way he felt right then—down, lonely, discouraged—he wasn't sure he could trust himself not to cry once again.

The river otters had noticed him and had stopped playing. They stared at him with wide-open eyes, watching to see what he was about to do.

Brewster hopped off his bicycle, aware of their gaze. He tried to seem nonchalant as he leaned the bicycle against a tree. He sauntered over to another tree with soft sand at its base, and got ready to stretch out for a rest.

He didn't notice the river otters nudging each other. It's too bad he didn't, because he might have realized that the place on which he was about to rest held a bad surprise for him in the form of a fire ant colony.

Most ants can bite. But the bite of a fire ant is like no other. It stings. It sends searing pain in every direction for a good long while. Being bitten by one fire ant is painful. Being bitten by a whole colony of them is almost unbearable. As soon as Brewster lay down under the tree, the biting began. Pain screamed through every nerve in his back. He leaped several feet into the air, yelping, still carrying a number of fire ants on his hide. "*Yowtch! Owtch! Ai! Ai! Ai!*" he screamed, jumping from one foot to another, trying to cool the burn. His entire back felt as if it was on fire, with new bites coming every second.

The river otters remained where they were, still watching the newcomer. A few of them began to chuckle at Brewster's pain. But one of them was more tenderhearted than the others. That river otter hushed his family. "Come on, now," he said. "That poor fellow is in pain. Remember when *I* was bitten by fire ants?"

The other river otters stopped guffawing and sighed. They did remember. They had all helped their little relation soothe his agony by applying mud packs and pouring cool water over his burning pelt. They looked at Brewster, still hopping in pain.

"Hey, Ferret," called the river otter who had once been bitten. "Come over here. I can help you. My name is Mike."

The stinging torture had begun to die down. Now Brewster was just sore all over. When he heard the first kind words directed toward him in hours, tears of gratitude welled up in his eyes.

Walking gingerly to where the river otters were clustered, Brewster said weakly, "Wow, that smarts. What *bit* me?"

"Those were fire ants," said Mike gently, approaching Brewster. "I'm sorry you had to find out about them the hard way. Come on over here. We'll put some mud on your back." He looked over at his relations. They were still standing a little ways away, looking at Brewster and now Mike. None of them came forward to help. "Oh, never mind," said Mike. "*I'll* put some mud on your back, anyway."

The other river otters went back to their games, forgetting about both Brewster and Mike. Brewster lay face down on the muddy bank, after carefully checking to make sure there were no fire ants around. Mike slapped mud over the most painful spots, talking soothingly to Brewster all the while. "You haven't had the easiest time making a home for yourself here, have you?" said Mike.

Wearily, Brewster shook his head. The problems he had faced since arriving at the Moustafaya Swamp made his heart feel heavy and sad. He said, "Oh, I'll be okay," not wanting to complain. But the catch in his voice as he spoke gave him away.

"We're not all so unfriendly, you know," said Mike. "It's just that nobody here is very used to outsiders. We've always lived here, just with each other."

The pain in Brewster's back had ebbed. But the pain in his heart was as great as ever. He sat up and looked at Mike. "I don't know exactly what made me come here," he said to the river otter. "I was drawn here by a feeling more powerful than anything I've ever felt before. Once I decided to come, nothing was going to stand in my way. I believe I'm supposed to be here. Sometimes I just wish I had been born and bred here, so I wouldn't have to go through all this misery."

"Do you want to come for a swim now?" said Mike. "The water would feel really good on your back."

Brewster looked over to where the other river otters were cavorting. He didn't want to go near them just then. "No thanks," he said, shaking his head. "Maybe some other time." He got back up on his bike. "But thanks for helping me out, Mike."

"Sure," said Mike, waving good-bye. "See you around, Ferret."

Brewster pedaled to his tent, his back still stinging, hunger rumbling through his stomach like a thunderstorm. "A trick around every corner, that's what's here," he said. But no bad tricks presented themselves as he rode home.

When he got there, he pulled out his last can of peas. "I'm so sick of peas I could spit," he thought as he got ready to open them. The chug of a motor in the distance stopped him. "Swamp Sallie!" he cried, racing down to the dock.

On this day, Sallie was dressed in a sparkling, sequined gown that dripped over the edges of her little boat, right into the waters of the Moustafaya Swamp. Little crawfish had attached themselves to its edges and were enjoying a ride. Every so often, Sallie lifted up the edges of her dress and plucked off the crawfish, popping them into a cast-iron pot that sat on the boat's bottom. "Hello there, Ferret!" she boomed. "How are you doing?"

"Better now!" said Brewster, all smiles.

"Did you eat your dinner yet?" asked Sallie. "I'm bringing you by some of my gumbo. It's the best in the whole of Bayou country!" She turned off her engine. Now her voice was so loud it made the leaves on the trees jiggle. "You haven't *lived* until you've eaten my gumbo." She heaved herself out of the boat and up the rickety dock, hauling her iron pot with her. "Now, don't just stand there gawking at me, Ferret," she thundered. "Make us a fire. We're going to have a *feast*."

Brewster ran for firewood, kindling, and matches, wondering at the way things seemed to perk up just when they looked as if they were as bad as they were ever going to get.

6

IN WHICH BREWSTER SAMPLES BAYOU COOKING
AND GETS HIS FIRST CUSTOMER

Sniff it up good before you try it, *cher*," said Swamp Sallie as she held a steaming bowl of gumbo up to Brewster.

Before he sniffed, Brewster peered inside the bowl. There were a lot of odd-looking things floating around in it.

Ferrets are simple creatures. They like their food plain and easy to identify. They are not what you would call adventurous eaters. That explains why Brewster was willing to eat canned peas day after day. A pea, now that's a food you could recognize at twenty paces. A pea is a pea. But what lurked in this bowl? Brewster stirred the rust-colored sauce, looking for some familiar food. He could make out a couple of crawfish tails. Then there were some plump, tan morsels he couldn't quite place. Brewster poked a bit farther with his spoon and saw that the bottom of the bowl was covered with rice. That, at least, was familiar. He scooped up a small spoonful of the rice and opened his mouth. Then he paused and looked at Sallie, a question in his eyes.

"It's hot, baby, it's hot," said Swamp Sallie, nodding. She had been watching Brewster's nervous exploration of his meal, grinning hugely. From time to time, low chortles would start up in her throat and then die down again.

Brewster pulled the spoon away from his mouth, squinted at it mistrustfully, looked back at Sallie, shrugged, squared his shoulders, and put the spoon in his mouth. Sallie leaned forward eagerly, her mouth agape, like a parent trying to get a baby to eat a mouthful of mush.

At first, the rice tasted like rice—nothing more, nothing less. Brewster chewed it tentatively. He swallowed it. Then the fire alarms went off inside his head. His tongue rolled up and back in surprise. His cheeks wiggled in and out. Tears rose to his eyes and filled them to the brim. His chin trembled. His lower lip wobbled.

"YEEEOOOOOOW!!!!" he shouted, bobbing his head from side to side, looking for anything to put in his mouth to cool it off. For a confused instant, he even eyed the mud at the edge of the water. His wild eyes sought Sallie's. How could his best friend in the whole of Moustafaya Swamp pull such a fast one on him?

Sallie poured a tall, cool glass of lemonade from her canteen and held it out to Brewster. "Drink this, baby," she said. "You'll cool down in a second."

Brewster drank. The lemonade did cool him down. "What is *in* there?" he demanded, panting.

"Oh, there's a little bit of my andouille, I suppose," mused Sallie. (That's how the name of the sausage is spelled. She pronounced it "ahn-dew-ee.") "And I put a few of those little crawfish in there, of course." She studied his bowl. "And rice. And onions. And peppers. And okra," she continued. "And, well, oh, I guess I used just a teeny bit of Tabasco sauce and red pepper, too."

"*Tabasco sauce?*" said Brewster. "Back where I come from, they use Tabasco sauce to bait rat traps!"

"Do tell," said Swamp Sallie, always genuinely interested to hear facts about distant places. "Well, hereabouts it's what we call our secret weapon. Now, tell me, Brewster, how do you like gumbo?"

Brewster recoiled at her question. His eyebrows shot up and down. How to answer? It was certainly the spiciest thing he had ever eaten. He ran his tongue over his lips. But now that the fire had died down, he realized that the little bite of rice *did* have a distinctive taste all its own. And even though just a couple of minutes before he had been hopping up and down in burning pain, now he was curious to have another taste—just a little one. "I think I'll try some more," he said, sifting around his bowl in search of something that was slightly recognizable.

"That's the boy," said Swamp Sallie. "First bite's always the hardest."

The next bite was easier. Maybe Brewster had already burned all of the feeling out of his mouth. He was emboldened to try a third bite, and a fourth, stopping only now and then for a sip of lemonade. "Hey, you know what? This is *good*," he said as he scooped up some okra and dropped it down his gullet. "My, that okra is tasty!"

"You're getting to be a real swamp fox, all right," said Swamp

Sallie, smiling, slapping her sides happily, and at last tucking into her own bowl of gumbo. After Brewster and Sallie had eaten for a few minutes, she looked at him out of the corner of her eye. "How's the messenger business going?" she asked.

Brewster sighed and told her the sad story of his morning. "Heaven's sake!" said Sallie, disgusted. "What's Cottonmouth doing sending you over to Hector's for a free radio advertisement? He'd never go along with that. Besides, you're competition for him. No, what you need to do is use word of mouth to build up your business."

"How'm I going to do that, Swamp Sallie?" said Brewster. "I can't even get my first customer."

"I'll have to think on that a spell," said Swamp Sallie ponderingly. After a minute's pause, she changed the subject instead. "You going to the Moustafaya Mix-up tonight?" she asked.

"It's the first I hear of it," said Brewster. "What is it?"

"Why, it's the best dancing of the year," said Swamp Sallie. "Everybody is there. Folks come from two or three swamps over. Birds fly in from everywhere. Why, some birds even come from South America. It's quite a party."

"Where is it held?" asked Brewster.

"It takes place in the big barn behind the wild boars' house," said Sallie. "It's too big a party for the Jolie Blonde Café to hold. You know, if you come there, you and I just might be able to do a two-step together. Though you'd better ask me quickly. My dance card fills up pretty fast."

Brewster wondered what it would be like to go to a party at the wild boars' barn. He wondered if they would even let him in.

How could such unfriendly-looking types host the biggest party anywhere around? Still, if Swamp Sallie was going to be there, things would probably be all right.

"I'd love to dance with you," Brewster told Sallie finally. "Will Wild Turkey and his group be there?"

"Will they *be* there! It's just the biggest night of the year for them, that's *all*," said Swamp Sallie. "They'll play like there's no tomorrow. You come on down. You'll see."

A call rang out. It sounded like this: *GABBLE-GOBBLE-GABBLE-GOBBLE-GABBLE.* "What is *that*?" said Brewster.

Sallie looked toward the sound and smiled. "I think Wild Turkey is looking for me," she said. "Want to come along and see him?"

"Do I ever!" said Brewster, hopping up so fast he turned his gumbo bowl over. It hardly mattered, for Brewster had finished every speck that was in there.

They hurried to Sallie's boat. She started the engine with a rip of the cord. They chugged to the Jolie Blonde Café.

"Where does Wild Turkey live?" asked Brewster.

"That's hard to say," said Swamp Sallie. "He travels around quite a bit. But most often he's nearby to the Jolie Blonde Café. He and Jolie Blonde are special friends," said Sallie, batting her eyelids and looking down demurely. "If you know what I mean."

Brewster remembered the elegant egret he had seen. He imagined that glamorous pair, dancing the night away at some romantic spot. "What a couple," he thought dreamily.

They puttered up to the pier at the Jolie Blonde Café. There stood Wild Turkey in despair. He was so upset, his feathers stood on end. His ruffle was mussed. His eyes flashed. His head shook from side to side.

When he saw them, he held up his accordion. Something terrible had happened to it. It was squeezed flatter than a pancake. Its buttons were busted. The fabric in the middle was torn and twisted. Even the band that held the accordian closed was

broken. "Sallie," moaned Wild Turkey, holding it out to her. "Look!"

"Oh, now, how did that happen?" said Swamp Sallie, clucking sadly. She leaped nimbly onto the dock and reached out to hold the damaged instrument. She cradled it like a baby and stood swaying as Wild Turkey broke into harsh sobs.

"That old wild boar—you know the one, Tommyrot?" said Wild Turkey, so angry he spit as he spoke. "He stepped on it! This squeeze-box was my daddy's. He gave it to me on his deathbed. Now what'm I gonna do? Tonight's the Moustafaya Mix-up. If I can't play my squeeze-box tonight, everything's gonna be ruined." And Wild Turkey sat right down on the dock and started sobbing.

Swamp Sallie, a furrow in her brow, asked, "Does anyone know if Happy Jack's Accordion Repair Shop is open today?"

"There's never any way of knowing," said Wild Turkey. "I heard the catfish are biting over at Bayou Lavalier. That can mean the shop will be closed for days while the old pig goes fishing."

"And there's no other place to go, is there?" said Swamp Sallie, shaking her head. "Not since Cousin Eddie's shop closed down."

"Yeah. Wasn't that a shame?" said Wild Turkey. "I liked dealing with Cousin Eddie quite a bit. And getting there wasn't such a terrible adventure." Wild Turkey looked knowingly at Swamp Sallie. They both nodded solemnly.

"Can't you take a ride up to Happy Jack's in your bus and see what's happening?" asked Sallie.

"Nope. The durn thing's out of commission. Brother

Dentelle—you know, the beaver in the band? He was parking it the other day and backed it up right into the swamp. Take a look," said Wild Turkey miserably. He pointed to the old bus. It was wedged in swamp mud almost up to its rear window.

Still in Sallie's boat, Brewster hung on their every word. In his mind, an idea had been born and was growing rapidly. Here was his first customer! He could take the accordion to Happy Jack's himself. Never mind that he had no idea where the place was. Hadn't he once ridden across an entire prairie dog town in South Dakota in one day? Wherever Happy Jack's was, Brewster would get there. And he would get that squeeze-box fixed. He would get it back in time for the Moustafaya Mix-up. He could do it. He swallowed a lump in his throat, took a deep breath, and said, "M-M-M-Mr. Turkey?"

Wild Turkey was so steeped in his misery that he took a moment to register Brewster's voice. He raised his head and looked around to see who had spoken. "Oh, hello," he said when he finally spotted Brewster in the boat. "Aren't you that little feller that came down here from Montana? How you doing?"

"That's South Dakota," said Brewster, feeling braver. He stepped out of the boat and onto the dock. "I think I'm the answer to your prayers. I happen to operate the Moustafaya Bicycle Messenger Service," he said proudly. "And I guarantee that I can get your accordion to Happy Jack's and bring it back in time for the Moustafaya Mix-up."

Wild Turkey looked skeptical. Swamp Sallie, standing behind Wild Turkey, shook her head. "You can't go there on a bicycle," she said.

"No way," said Wild Turkey.

"I can do it!" said Brewster.

"You see," said Swamp Sallie, "first you've got to get out to the main highway. Now, that takes some doing. Once you're there, you've got to go five miles farther. Happy Jack's is at the end of a long, straight road with no turns off it whatsoever. But that's not your biggest problem. On that road live the Bayou Bloodhounds, the most vicious curs ever seen on this earth. You'd never get past them alive."

"I'm even afraid to go by them in my bus!" agreed Wild Turkey.

Brewster was undaunted. Wild Turkey needed him. "Give me a chance. What have you got to lose?"

Swamp Sallie said kindly, "We could lose *you*, Brewster. And I'm just beginning to get used to having you around here."

"You know, Sallie," said Wild Turkey. "Those curs *do* take an afternoon nap. Maybe the ferret will be able to sneak by them while they're sleeping."

"Maybe," said Sallie, thinking. She went back to her boat and reached under the stern seat, where she usually sat. She pulled out a big perfume bottle, the old-fashioned type that sprays perfume with a squeeze bulb. "Maybe you can squirt some of this Eau de Gator on yourself, *cher*," she said. "They *may* leave you alone if they think you're an alligator. And they're so *dumb*, you just might be able to fool them."

"It's worth a try, don't you think?" said Brewster, very excited.

Swamp Sallie and Wild Turkey looked at each other. Clearly, this ferret was determined. They grimaced, shrugged their shoulders, and agreed, "It's worth a try."

"*Yahoo!*" said Brewster. "I'm in business!"

Wild Turkey handed him the accordion. "Now, be careful of this, son. It was my daddy's."

"I will be, sir," said Brewster, carefully taking the instrument. "And I'll come through for you. Believe me, I will."

Swamp Sallie and Brewster hopped back into the boat. The engine started up with its usual cloud of blue smoke.

"He just might come through, at that," said Wild Turkey, pulling thoughtfully on his red wattles as he watched the little boat putt away.

7

IN WHICH BREWSTER TRAVELS
TO HAPPY JACK'S ACCORDION SHOP

Before he set out on his trip, Brewster stuck Swamp Sallie's perfume bottle in one of his jersey pockets. He filled his water bottle from a little spring he had lately discovered behind his campsite and put it in the cage on his bicycle frame.

When he was ready to go, he went down to the dock and called for Swamp Sallie. "Hallo-o-o-o-o-o-o!" he shouted, his voice echoing over the still waters. She soon chugged into sight. She looked him up and down, and said, "Now you listen here. Nobody is going to think you're a coward if you change your mind about this trip. I don't know one single soul in this whole entire swamp who would be willing to go to Happy Jack's on a bicycle. Not *anybody*. Those Bayou Bloodhounds are as vicious as they come." Her voice lowered to a whisper as she continued. "If you decide not to go, nobody even has to know that you were fool enough to offer to make the trip. Wild Turkey and I would never say a word."

Though Brewster listened to his friend, his mind was made up. The chance to be a hero to Wild Turkey, and so to all of the creatures of the swamp, was too great to resist. He knew the trip was dangerous, but he tried not to think about that. He forced himself to think of the end of the journey, when he would return with Wild Turkey's accordion fixed and ready to go, just in time for the Moustafaya Mix-up. "Thanks for everything, Sallie," said Brewster, his voice steady, his jaw set tightly. "I'll be okay."

Swamp Sallie shook her head. "I don't know," she said sadly. She was quiet for a minute. Then she gave up. "I guess it's your choice." She shrugged her shoulders. "Good luck."

Brewster picked up Wild Turkey's damaged accordion. "How am I going to carry this thing?" he wondered, scratching his head. The accordion had a leather strap on one end. Brewster slid the strap up over his shoulder and heaved the accordion onto his back. It was heavy, but it felt all right. He discovered one strange effect right away: Whenever he swayed from side to side, air entered the accordion, causing it to wheeze and whine loudly. "I'll just have to try not to weave," Brewster thought.

As he lifted one leg over the seat and hopped on his bicycle, Brewster thought about his family. If his mother were there, what would she do? He pondered, then decided she would look into his eyes, hug him, and say, "Do what you think is right, son."

"I am, Mother," whispered Brewster as he started pedaling. "This is just one more part of the adventure."

Brewster rode past Cottonmouth, who was sunning herself on a tree stump by the river. "Where are you going, Ferret?" she drawled, her voice lazy and slow, relaxed by the hot sun. Brewster almost told her. She *was* one of his few friends in the Moustafaya Swamp. But the fewer folks he told about his excursion, the less

explaining he would have to do later—in case it didn't work out. "Oh hi, Cottonmouth!" he said, a tad too cheerily, trying to keep his bicycle steady so that the accordion would stay quiet. "Just going for a ride; that's all." He hoped that his tone of voice was convincing and that Cottonmouth wouldn't lift her head enough to notice the broken accordion which clung to his back.

Cottonmouth lifted her head a little from the tree stump and examined Brewster. If she noticed the accordion (and she could hardly have missed it), she had the decency not to mention it. She lowered her head and said, "Happy trails, Ferret. Until we meet again." She shut her eyes and resumed her nap.

Brewster hoped sincerely that he would be able to get onto the Moustafaya Trail without running into anybody else. He especially did not want to see Hector Raccoon nor any of his nosy family. As he rode past Hector's store, he was relieved to find its porch empty. But he was so busy looking at the store, he didn't watch where he was riding. His front wheel bumped right over a rock in the middle of the path.

Brewster didn't crash—just almost. But he did jiggle the accordion a little. It gave off a mournful *Hunh-heeeee*. Naturally, all of Hector's family, and Hector himself, ran onto the porch to see what had caused the commotion. "Think fast, Ferret," Brewster whispered urgently to himself. "Think fast."

"What on earth are you doing?" asked Hector, his arms folded tightly across his chest, a sharp toothpick sticking out of the corner of his mouth. On either side of him stood his sons, in exactly the same position. They were ready for a good laugh. Brewster was determined it wouldn't be at his expense.

He decided to tell the truth, though not the whole truth. "I'm doing my bicycle messenger work," he told Hector. "Business is booming," he added blithely. "Couldn't be better!" He pedaled away quickly, carefully avoiding any other impediments in his path.

When Brewster hit the Moustafaya Trail, he began to pick up speed. He was glad to be riding and to see trees, bushes, birds, and scenery fly past. His heart beat more rapidly, and his blood sped through his veins.

Before long, he was back at the wild boars' house. The boars were headed toward their barn, pushing wheelbarrows full of party decorations. One wheelbarrow held paper lanterns. Another held brightly colored party lights. Against the barn

MOUSTAFAYA MIX-UP
TONIGHT AT 8:00

leaned a large sign that read Moustafaya Mix-up: Tonight at 8 o'clock. The boars glanced at Brewster as he rode past with Wild Turkey's accordion on his back.

The biggest, ugliest, meanest-looking boar of them all gaped at Brewster, his tusks twinkling in the sunlight. "That must be Tommyrot," thought Brewster. "If this works out, I'll have him to thank. And he'll have me to thank, too." Brewster didn't let himself think about what he would do or how he would feel if it didn't work out.

Since the boars already knew about the broken accordion, Brewster decided to show off a little. "Running this up to Happy Jack's," he called with a cheery wave of his hand that took in the broken accordion. "Don't worry. I'll have it back in time for the Mix-up."

Tommyrot actually waved at Brewster. "Good luck with the hounds, Ferret," he called in a gruff voice that sounded as if it didn't get used very often.

Brewster rode along the main highway, looking for the turnoff to Twenty Mile Road. The countryside was flat. He could see for miles in every direction. Here and there, twisted trees stuck up from muddy riverbeds. Stands of water sparkled in the afternoon sunshine. The sky was hazy, the air was warm and moist. There was almost no traffic on the road, though occasionally an old truck loaded with furniture, or a small, beaten-up car with muffler problems, zoomed past, heading north.

The empty highway suited Brewster just fine. As he sped along, he sang a song that his Uncle Rex had taught him when he was just a kit, long before he ever got his bicycle.

Oh, the world is such a beautiful place,
It's filled with wonderful things.
I hope to see the wide, wide world,
And travel, and visit, and sing.

The chorus was his favorite part:

Oh, hee, hee, HI, you wonderful world,
How do you like me now?
Oh, he, he, HIIIII, you marvelous place,
How do you like me now?

Brewster sang that chorus over and over. Each time he sang it, he would say the word "HI" louder and longer, until it became a drawn-out howl. He threw his head back, squeezed his eyes shut, and opened his mouth as wide as it would go, filling the day with his happy shout.

"Twenty Mile Road," said Brewster, reading the ramshackle sign with the arrow that pointed right. He took a deep breath. "Well," he said, blowing the air back out of his lungs. "Here we go."

As Brewster made the sharp right turn onto Twenty Mile Road, the accordion took a deep breath, too. *Hunnh-eeee*, it moaned.

"You hush now!" scolded Brewster, looking over his shoulder at the ruined instrument.

Twenty Mile Road was straight and flat. On either side, all Brewster could see were empty fields of dried brown grass, and ahead he saw nothing but the ribbon of road. Where the road dipped here and there, Brewster thought he saw puddles of water. But he knew that it hadn't rained lately and that the puddles were just mirages.

He was glad he could see so far in the distance. "I hope I'll be able to take those bloodhounds by surprise," he thought. Just mentioning their name gave Brewster the willies. Back in South Dakota, dogs were the biggest enemy a ferret could ever have. In fact, nobody even knew there were black-footed ferrets at all until a German shepherd named Shep found one, killed it, and brought it back to his master. Until then, black-footed ferrets had enjoyed great privacy out on the prairie, minding their own business. Once Shep discovered them, things were terrible for a while. Everyone went ferret-crazy, trying to find all the black-footed ferrets and put metal tags on their ears.

Though this had happened before Brewster was even born, the stories of this horror were very familiar to him, as his family had whispered them again and again to him and his sisters and brothers as they huddled in their den. As a result, Brewster and all the black-footed ferrets were uncommonly leery of dogs.

But Brewster was determined not to let the Bayou Bloodhounds get the better of him. Swamp Sallie had told him that the bloodhounds lived in a hollow at the bottom of Racketty Hill. "It's called Racketty Hill because Twenty Mile Road is in such pitiful shape over there," explained Sallie. "Anything that goes down the hill makes a terrible sound." Brewster worried about the sound the accordion was likely to make as he biked down that hill. He practiced riding with his back very straight and still. He watched the road ahead of him.

Finally, up ahead, he saw that the road was about to dip *way* down. "Racketty Hill," he whispered, his mouth suddenly dry. Lucky for him, there was a little breeze in his face. He hoped it would keep the bloodhounds from recognizing his scent too soon. He slowed way down and pulled out his water bottle, taking a long swig as he surveyed the situation.

Though Racketty Hill was long, it was not very steep. It sloped down into a dusty little hollow. Peering ahead, Brewster spied a farmhouse, its yard littered with broken-down automobiles. He craned his neck and squinted his eyes. He didn't see any hounds, at least not right away.

Then he saw them: four big dogs with floppy ears lying on top

of one another in a heap. Just as Wild Turkey had predicted, they were asleep.

"Might be time for a little help from my friend," thought Brewster as he reached into his jersey pocket and pulled out Swamp Sallie's Eau de Gator perfume. Lifting his chin, he pointed the bottle and squeezed the big rubber bulb. A cold liquid with a strange smell squirted all over his neck. Sniffing it a few times, Brewster had to admit that it *did* smell just a little bit like Swamp Sallie and her relations.

Brewster looked down at the hounds again. He thought of his mother. He thought of all his family, and of Swamp Sallie and Cottonmouth. Most of all, he thought of Wild Turkey. "Here I go," he whispered, as loudly as he dared. Even though the breeze was in his favor, he knew that bloodhounds have good ears *and* good noses.

He started pedaling faster. A tiny flutter of fear passed through him. "Come *on!*" he chided himself. "This will be *fun!*" As he sped down the hill, he almost believed himself.

8

IN WHICH BREWSTER
HURTLES DOWN RACKETTY HILL
TO FACE THE BAYOU BLOODHOUNDS

Racketty Hill's roadway was worn and full of pot-holes, bumps, and lumps. But Brewster was such a good bicycle rider that he knew how to skirt these pitfalls. He concentrated on keeping his back straight so the accordion wouldn't wheeze and wake up the Bayou Bloodhounds.

Every few seconds, Brewster squinted his eyes up ahead to where the dogs lay sleeping. As he got closer, he could make them out very clearly.

They were big. To Brewster, they looked enormous. Their dark bodies were bony. Each was a different color—one tan, one gray, one beige, and one dark brown. Their fur looked worn and moth-eaten. Their long ears spread out on either side of their heads, looking like dusty carpets on the hard-baked clay soil. Their tails were long and skinny. As they slept, they all breathed at the same time, their sides rising and falling. Except for that movement, they were still.

"I'm lucky they're asleep," Brewster thought. He rode carefully, sending the dogs mental messages. "Lullaby, doggies," he thought. "Sweet dreams."

Brewster had worked up quite a bit of speed as he zoomed down Racketty Hill. He was cruising so quickly down the hill that he stopped pedaling for a moment, letting the bicycle coast and enjoying the dangerous feeling of sneaking by the vicious dogs. He was gliding right up to them. He could see the drool dripping out of the corners of their mouths, hear the heavy sound of their breathing. Just as he went past them, he turned his head for a close-up peek. And that is when it happened. A pebble, not much bigger than a quarter, lay in the middle of the road, right in Brewster's path. His front tire went over it with a bump. The bump made the accordion hop up and down on Brewster's back. It wheezed loudly: *Hunh-wheeenh!*

The four hounds' heads shot up. Their noses searched the air— but only for an instant—and settled immediately on Brewster. They stared at him with stupid eyes.

"Ride, ride, ride," chanted Brewster to himself, his body electric with fear. "Ride, boy, ride." He sent all his strength into his legs, and pushed the pedals faster and faster.

The bloodhounds were quick, too. They leaped to their feet and took off after Brewster, baying like banshees. They loped like hungry jackrabbits, their clumsy legs churning up dust from the roadway, their heavy paws thudding on the ground. Their huge, wet tongues dangled out of the sides of their mouths.

Brewster rode for his life. His head hung low over the handlebars, his eyes looked straight ahead. His breath came hot and dry, straining with effort. His throat grew parched, his tongue stick-

ing to the top of his mouth. He knew the bloodhounds were gain-
ing on him with every second. Soon he could feel their hot breath
at his heels.

Just ahead, Brewster saw a tumbledown building with a hand-
lettered sign: Happy Jack's Accordion Shop. His heart leaped. It
leaped again when a mastiff that looked as big as a small truck
stood up on the porch of the shop and barked furiously at the
Bayou Bloodhounds. They let up their pace and fell back, whim-
pering. They had reached the edge of their territory. Brewster
dared to look back over his shoulder. He saw the bloodhounds
returning unhappily to their own rattletrap homestead.

"Wow!" breathed Brewster, putting on his brakes and coming
to a stop. He glanced worriedly at the mastiff, wondering if he
had a new enemy to confront.

But the big dog, apparently satisfied that the Bayou Bloodhounds had not ventured onto his turf, collapsed happily on the porch and laid his huge head down on his paws with something like a smile on his face.

"*Whew!*" said Brewster, hopping off his bicycle. He sat down on the top porch step and panted hard for several minutes, his heart thumping in triple time. Then he pulled out his water bottle and took a good, long drink, wiping his mouth on his sleeve when he finished.

9

IN WHICH BREWSTER MEETS HAPPY JACK

When his eyes could focus again and when his pulse had stopped pounding in his ears, Brewster glanced at the mastiff. The dog was scratching at some fleas behind his ear, quite unconcerned about Brewster's presence. So Brewster looked around.

He sat on a splintery porch that fronted an old wooden house. The house may have once been painted white, but time and muddy rainwater had turned it an all-over grayish-brown color. The wall of the house directly behind the porch consisted mainly of a dirty glass window, cracked in places and patched with dingy tape. On the window were hand-painted the words Happy Jack's Accordion Repair Emporium. We Work While You Wait. No Job Too Big or Too Small.

A dusty window shade was drawn over the window. Brewster tried to peek around the edges to get a feeling for the place, but all was dark inside. The shop's front door was half wood and half glass. Both were painted black. Tacked to the front door was a sign lettered in the same crooked writing as the sign in the window. It read Gone Fishing.

"Oh, no!" said Brewster, reeling in frustration with this piece of bad news. "I can't believe it!"

The mastiff slowly lifted his heavy head and looked quizzical. "What's all the fuss about?" he asked. He had the sleepiest voice Brewster had ever heard.

"I've got to find Mr. Happy Jack," said Brewster anxiously, unslinging the accordion from his shoulder and waving it as he spoke. "I've got Wild Turkey's accordion here. I have to get it back to the boars' barn in time for the Moustafaya Mix-up. That's *tonight!*" Nervously, he looked at the sun. It had begun to sink just a little in the sky. He put the time at about two-thirty. There wasn't a minute to waste.

If the dog was affected in any way by Brewster's air of urgency, it was hard to tell. He lay his head heavily back on his paws and breathed slowly and loudly for a minute or two. Brewster was afraid that the dog was falling asleep again. But then the mastiff lifted his head and said, "Well, I might *could* show you where Happy Jack is fishing. 'Course, if the catfish are biting, there's *nothing* going to get him back into the shop until he's good and ready."

"He's just *got* to come back and fix this," moaned Brewster.

"Maybe he will and maybe he won't," said the dog. "I will make no promises." He rose slowly to his feet and, with a jerk of his head, said, "Come on now." He ambled toward a nearby clump of trees.

Brewster wondered whether to carry the accordion along or not. He decided that showing the broken instrument to Happy Jack would be the best way to get him back into his shop pronto. Brewster slung the accordion over his shoulder, and nervously followed the big, old dog.

The mastiff didn't seem inclined to talk, so Brewster held his tongue until curiosity overcame him, and he risked a question. "What made the Bayou Bloodhounds lay off chasing me?" he asked.

The mastiff chuckled. "Those old hounds and I have been

barking at each other for as long as we've known *how* to bark," he said. "There're no angry words we haven't exchanged. But we're all dogs together. We have a line between our two properties, and we all know where it is. They know that, old as I am, I could take on all four of them at the same time. 'Course, it's different for you," he continued, glancing at Brewster. "You're kinda small. And now that they've seen you once, they're going to be waiting for you." He shook his head. "You're not even a dog, are you?" he said. "Just what kind of animal are you, anyway?"

"I'm a ferret—a black-footed ferret," said Brewster, deciding not to go into further explanations.

"Well, you're going to have quite a time of it on your way back to Moustafaya Swamp, that's for sure," said the mastiff, shaking his big, shaggy head. "I don't envy you the trip."

Brewster sighed. "Let's just take this one step at a time," he said. "First I've got to see about getting the accordion fixed."

They reached the bank of a sleepy river. Beneath the shade of a spreading oak tree, atop a checkered cloth, accompanied by a huge wicker picnic basket, lounged Happy Jack, fishing intently.

Happy Jack was a pig. He was the biggest pig Brewster had ever seen—and Brewster had once watched the pig-judging at the South Dakota State Fair, so he knew a big pig when he saw one. Happy Jack's big fat self almost completely covered the checkered cloth on which he sat. He was well dressed, in an old-fashioned way, complete with a three-button vest. Each of the buttons strained with the effort of holding the two sides of the vest together without popping off like champagne corks. The vest had a pocket from which peeped a twinkling gold watch fob.

Happy Jack wore a white shirt, which was surprisingly immaculate, and a black string tie. He wore short-legged pants called knickers, argyle socks, and black shoes with spats. (Brewster had never actually seen spats before, but his Uncle Rex once described them when he told a story about the time the first automobile had driven through the prairie dog town near Brewster's home.)

The pig's face was as round and uncreased as a baby's. His smiling eyes were squinty-shut. He seemed the picture of contentment. He held a fishing pole, its line dangling in the slow-moving river. At the same time, he ate small, delicate chocolate candies. "Hello there," he said in a voice as smooth as silk. "Now, what have we here?"

The mastiff grunted, "Customer, Jack." He nodded at Brewster and then turned around and shuffled slowly back toward the house.

Brewster called to the dog, "Thanks!" But the dog didn't turn around. He was probably most intent on picking up his nap where he had left it off some minutes before.

Brewster turned back to Happy Jack. Brewster wasn't sure how to start up a conversation with him. So he waited. After a few silent moments, he held out the tattered accordion and flashed a tight little smile. "Wild Turkey needs this fixed by tonight," he said in a small voice. "Can you help?"

"*Ssh! Ssh!*" said Happy Jack, heeding his fishing line, which had begun to twitch. He turned his full attention to the river and began to reel in. Within a couple of minutes, he had pulled in a big, old rubber boot, which he detached disgustedly before turning back to Brewster and reaching for the accordion with a sigh. "Let me see it; let me see it."

Brewster handed over the squeeze-box. Happy Jack turned it all around and shook his head, amazed. "I don't think I've ever *seen* something as wrecked up as this!" he said. "How on earth did this happen?"

"Tommyrot the boar stepped on it," explained Brewster.

"And how'd you get to be unlucky enough to bring it clear over here?" asked Happy Jack.

"I operate the Moustafaya Bicycle Messenger Service," said Brewster, his voice ringing with pride. "Something like this is all in a day's work," he added, shrugging his shoulders with what he hoped was an air of unconcern.

"You rode by those bloodthirsty hounds on a *bicycle?*" said Happy Jack with a low, amazed whistle. "That's something, all righty all right. Well, if you did that for Wild Turkey, the least I can do is see about fixing this here accordion. Help me up." He reached toward Brewster, who helped him stand.

Meticulously, Happy Jack brushed crumbs off his vest, handed Brewster his fishing pole, and reached for the accordion. "Why don't you sit here by the river and see if you can collect me a few catfish for supper? I'll go get to work."

Brewster was pleased. "Thanks, Mr. Jack."

"That's Happy Jack, son," said the pig with a kindly smile. "Bad as this thing looks, I should be able to fix it in time. You just sit back and relax. You're going to have to store up your strength for the trip back." The big pig shuffled to the shop, carrying the accordion.

Brewster leaned against the big, old oak tree, after carefully checking its base for fire ants. He sighed and picked up the fishing pole.

Maybe it was the effort he had already spent that afternoon in just getting to where he was. Maybe it was the Louisiana heat that made him feel lazy. But as soon as Brewster sat under the tree and got comfortable, he fell asleep.

For a long time, he slept motionless, dreamless. Then a dream began. He was with his family again. But Uncle Rex wasn't there. "Where is Uncle Rex?" Brewster asked his mother in the dream.

"He went off to see the world," she said, smiling sadly. "But he ran into some hungry dogs." She shook her head, tears flowing. "He didn't make it."

"Oh, no!" said Brewster. "Couldn't he have protected himself?"

"That's the funny thing of it," said his mother. "He knew those bad dogs were there. But he went right on up to them, anyway. And after all those stories he always told you about dogs, too! Don't *you* ever get stuck running into a pack of dogs," she warned him.

Brewster awoke with a start. The afternoon had passed very quickly. The sun was soon going to set. "Oh, no!" he cried, leaping to his feet. He raced to Happy Jack's shop and banged the door open.

There were all sorts of animals sitting around in there. Brewster spotted a turtle, a fox, a couple of raccoons, a beaver, and a salamander. They sat in a circle, perched on boxes, barrels, and a few broken-down chairs. In the middle of the circle was Happy Jack, about to play Wild Turkey's accordion, now fixed as good as new. "Hello there, Ferret," he called cheerily. "I think we're all set!" He began to play.

Happy Jack's style was different from Wild Turkey's, whose songs were always full of sorrow, hope, and high emotion. Happy Jack's music was lighthearted and giddy. The notes of the song rose out of the instrument like dancers, gliding through the air as though they rode on fluff-covered milkweed seeds, bouncing against each other and floating out to the sky.

The music made all the animals want to move. First they bobbed their heads. Next they moved their arms and legs. Then they were all up dancing with each other, round and round in small circles, their feet flying with joy. "Wah-hoo!" called a beaver. "Hoo-ee!" answered a fox.

Happy Jack played and played, his eyes closed, his big head bobbing back and forth. Though at first he was too worried about getting the accordion back to enjoy what he was hearing, Brewster was soon pulled into the joyous sound, just like everyone else. He twitched in time with the music, and then his body started to move, all by itself. He went into the center of the group and began to twirl round and stomp his feet, dancing joyously and joining the other animals in their calls.

Finally, Happy Jack stopped playing and handed the accordion to Brewster. It still felt warm from the pig's touch. "I think you're in business, little feller," said Happy Jack to Brewster. "Now, get back on your bicycle and ride like the wind. You'll get back in time . . . *if* you make it." He said this last with his voice dropped down low. The other animals, understanding his tone, all looked at Brewster with sympathy.

"I'll make it back," said Brewster. "I have to. Wild Turkey is depending on me. *Everyone* is depending on me."

10

BREWSTER'S COURAGE

Nervously eyeing the sinking sun, Brewster stepped off the porch at Happy Jack's and got his bicycle ready to ride. Happy Jack and all the other animals followed him outside. As Brewster climbed on his bike, he slung the repaired accordion over his shoulder and grinned at Happy Jack. "What do we owe you?" asked Brewster.

"Tell Wild Turkey this one's on me," said Happy Jack with a gentle smile. "Good luck."

The other animals waved good-bye solemnly. They knew what Brewster was about to face. Worst of all, they knew that at this time of day, the Bayou Bloodhounds would be hungry for their dinner. It was bad enough trying to outride *sleepy* bloodhounds when riding *down* Racketty Hill. It was hard to imagine what would happen to Brewster when he had to outride *hungry* blood-hounds while going *up* Racketty Hill.

Nobody spoke, but several of the animals silently stepped up to Brewster and squeezed his shoulder.

Brewster himself was strangely calm. He thought only of the

end of his ride—of helping Wild Turkey and all of the animals at Moustafaya Swamp. He thought of how their faces would look when he arrived with Wild Turkey's accordion. "I can't think about what lies between now and then," he thought. "I just can't."

"What are you gonna do about those *dogs?*" asked Happy Jack finally, tilting his head to one side and looking Brewster in the eye.

Brewster looked squarely back at him. "I'll think of something," he said. With a wave, a smile, and a slight, friendly nod, Brewster bid farewell to Happy Jack and all of the other animals. "It was a real pleasure to meet all of you," he said.

"Good luck, Brewster," they called.

Brewster pedaled away from Happy Jack's. He peeked over his shoulder as he moved out onto the road. The animals stood motionless, looking after him. Happy Jack called out, "Brewster, keep your courage!"

Happy Jack's last words broadened the smile on Brewster's face and gave him strength. "Courage," he repeated, tasting that delicious word in his mouth. "I have courage!" Mulling this over, he breathed deeply, wondering how to overcome his enemies.

Before he got to the Bayou Bloodhound's farmhouse, Brewster stopped and stood over his bike for a moment, looking ahead. About two hundred yards away, the four dogs paced, waiting for him to exit the mastiff's territory and enter theirs. "Those dogs are ready for me, all right," Brewster thought. "But I'm not quite ready for them. What am I going to do?" A flicker of fear threatened his resolve.

At that instant, he spied a big, old board lying in the grass. He remembered a story Uncle Rex had told him about the way knights in the Middle Ages rode into battle, swinging their heavy broadswords over their heads. "That's it!" he shouted, snatching the board and hopping back on his bike. He was ready.

Soon Brewster was tooling along at a high speed, swinging the heavy board in a circle over his head. "Here I come!" he roared. He trembled with courage. His soul flooded with excitement. Brewster was so full of feelings, he thought he would burst. He had to let some of those feelings out.

"EEEEEEYAAAAAAAAA!" he hollered. It felt so good, he said it again, even louder and longer: "EEEEEEEEEEEEEEEEE-YAAAAAAAAAAAAAA!" His whoops were wilder than anything he had ever heard—even at the Jolie Blonde Café. Brewster hollered so loudly that he drowned out the baying of the bloodhounds . . . at least in his own ears.

But nothing could blot out the sight of them. The tan and the

gray bloodhounds galloped toward him at full speed, their mouths wide open, their slavering tongues lolling out, their eyes glowing like coals. "A-A-A-OOO!" they howled, their combined calls deafening. "A-A-A-OOO!"

Brewster's eyes narrowed to slits. *"You can't stop me!"* he cried. The two dogs reached the bicycle. They leaped. Brewster could smell their foul breath and gaze into their empty, starving eyes. He swung the board at their heads with menace. Surprised, they fell over backward, cringing. Clumsily, they righted themselves and ran some distance away from him, whining.

"EEEEEEEEYAAAAAA!" screamed Brewster. "Two down! Two to go!"

The beige bloodhound ran a little behind the other two. He saw what had happened to his mates, but he was loping too fast to slow down. Maybe he ran just a little faster, determined that this little animal wouldn't get the best of *all* of them. He gnashed his sharp teeth, preparing to pounce on the ferret.

Brewster swung the board several times overhead, then launched it like a boomerang, aimed at the dog's long, skinny legs. The board landed squarely on target, tripping the hound and sending him skittering, tumbling head over heels in a confounded lump.

"Three down!" screamed Brewster. *"Nothing can stop me now!"*

The brown bloodhound was waiting for Brewster. So was the bottom of Racketty Hill, looming large in the growing darkness. Brewster no longer held the board. He had to ride straight up the hill to get to safety. But he was not afraid. "I can do it! I can do it!" he chanted. He spun the pedals faster and faster.

The dog chased Brewster, barking and howling, his a-a-a-ooo's echoed by the other dogs, who had righted themselves and resumed the chase, as well. "Go! Go! Go! Go!" Brewster chanted, his heart thundering in his chest.

The faster the fourth bloodhound ran, the faster Brewster rode. The bicycle wheels whirled so quickly that the spokes were a blur. "Up! Up! *Up!*" said Brewster, rising higher and higher up Racketty Hill.

"A-A-A-OOOO!" howled the bloodhound, so close to Brewster's tail that he could feel the dog's hot breath and could feel the ground shake under the weight of the dog's galloping body. But surge after surge of strength powered Brewster, and he pedaled faster and faster. When he reached the top of Racketty Hill, he sprinted for a few more minutes. Then he listened.

He heard no more baying. He heard no more pounding feet. The fourth bloodhound had given up the chase. Brewster was alone.

"EEEEEEEEEEEEYAAAAAAAAAAAAAA!" shouted Brewster. "I DID IT!"

He was so happy, he rode on at top speed, mile after mile. By now, night had fallen. The darkness was complete. Brewster switched on the light on the front of his bicycle. It threw a beam that served as a beacon, pointing directly to the wild boars' barn.

Meanwhile, back at the barn, the crowd had gathered for the Moustafaya Mix-up. There were swamp creatures of every description, decked out in their finest garb. The river otters, their fur slicked back with pine tar, stood at one side of the room, preening one another. Tompkin the pelican, elegant in a cutaway and top hat, squired his lady friend around the crowded floor. Birds filled the rafters. Lizards, snakes, and salamanders clung to the walls and posts. Nutrias stood in silent pairs, ready to dance, their faces blank.

Wild Turkey, Tommyrot, and Swamp Sallie had decided not to tell anybody what Brewster was up to. They were frantic with worry. "Oh, my. Oh, my. Imagine that poor little animal going through all that for *me!*" fretted Wild Turkey.

"It was all my fault," wailed Tommyrot. "*I should have been the one to go.*"

Swamp Sallie, dressed in her party finest, a handsome black veil covering her face, narrowed her eyes at the sniveling boar. "You couldn't ride a bicycle to save your life, much less to *risk* it!" she said dryly. To Wild Turkey she said, "I just hope our friend is all right."

Cottonmouth, her face filled with concern, slithered up to Swamp Sallie. "Where's Brewster?" she asked. "He headed off right after lunch, and he hasn't been back all day. I thought we'd come here together, but I haven't been able to find him."

Swamp Sallie said evenly, "He took Wild Turkey's accordion to Happy Jack's."

"On a *bicycle?*" said Cottonmouth, her jaw dropping in shock. "How could he? What about the bloodhounds?"

"He insisted," explained Swamp Sallie.

"There was nothing we could do to stop him," said Wild Turkey.

"He should have been back a long time ago," said Tommyrot, starting to sob. "I'm just worried sick about him."

Behind them, Hector Raccoon was eavesdropping on the conversation. His eyes widened in surprise when he heard what was going on. "Unbelievable!" he said. He hurried to tell his family the news.

"Uh-oh," said Swamp Sallie as she watched Hector start to spread the story.

Quickly, they told Jolie Blonde what was happening. "We'd better make some sort of an announcement," said the egret, dabbing her handkerchief at the corner of one of her black, beady eyes. (She always cried when she was anxious.) "I can't do it, Wild Turkey," she said. "I'm too upset."

"I'll do it," said Wild Turkey. Clearing his throat, he went to the microphone. The crowd howled when they saw him, and then they fell silent.

"You're probably wondering why the music hasn't started yet," said Wild Turkey. "That's because we're waiting for the safe return of one of the bravest souls I have ever known. This year's Moustafaya Mix-up was almost called off. This morning, my accordion was smashed to smithereens—by accident," he added, glaring at Tommyrot, who hung his head in shame. "Now, there's a new little feller around these parts. Maybe some of you have had the good fortune to meet him. His name is Brewster Ferret. When he saw that accordion, he said, 'I'll take it to Happy Jack's for you on my bicycle, Wild Turkey!' I said to him, 'No, no, you can't do *that*. Not on a bicycle!'"

"The bloodhounds! The bloodhounds!" murmured the crowd.

"That's right! I told him about the bloodhounds. Sure I did," continued Wild Turkey. "But he wouldn't hear any of it. 'I'm going,' he said. 'I'll be back with your accordion in time for the mix-up.'"

"Brave!" spoke the crowd. "What courage!" they called.

"Well, Brewster should have been back by now," said Wild Turkey. "And to be honest with you, we're getting just a mite bit worried about him. In fact, in just a little while I think I'm going to head up the road myself—on foot—to see what's become of him. And while I'm gone looking for him, I want each of you to send him your thoughts, your wishes, and your best hopes. For this ferret, this newcomer, this stranger in our midst, is as good a neighbor and friend as any of you is ever going to meet."

"Here is your accordion, Wild Turkey," said Brewster, walking through the door.

"BREWSTER!" shouted Wild Turkey, enveloping him in a hug that left the ferret gasping for breath.

The crowd roared. Animals hopped into the air. Birds swooped from the rafters. Snakes slithered up posts. They chanted, "*Brewster! Brewster! Brewster! Brewster!*"

Swamp Sallie grabbed Brewster away from Wild Turkey and locked him in an embrace, too. "You did it, you little son of a gun!" she shouted. "You did it. I'm so proud of you!"

Brewster looked down at his feet. He was pretty proud of himself, too.

"*Speech! Speech! Speech!*" hollered everyone.

Brewster looked around the barn. Suddenly, all of them, even

those who had treated him as an outsider, who had turned their backs on him, now seemed like friends. Hector Raccoon caught Brewster's eye from the back of the barn and gave a friendly wave, dipping his head to say hello.

Brewster was not a born public speaker. But he did have something he wanted to say to the crowd. He stepped up to the microphone. "This morning, when I woke up, I felt like a stranger here. It's been a long day. But I'm finally home. And I don't feel like a stranger anymore."

"*Hurray!*" shouted the crowd. They cheered for five full minutes. Then Wild Turkey handed Brewster a giant iron triangle and a stick to hit it with—just like the one Brewster had seen in his dream the night before. "We'd like you to join the band, little feller," he said. "Would you do us the honor?"

"Would I ever!" said Brewster, clanging his triangle and beaming with pride.

That Moustafaya Mix-up was the best one ever. Folks around the swamp still talk about it to this day. And from that moment on, Brewster Ferret was an honored resident of the community. His Moustafaya Messenger Service was such a success that he eventually had to teach Mike the river otter how to ride a bicycle, too, just to keep up with the business. Mike was a pretty good worker, though he often overslept when he took his afternoon nap.

Once his business got going, Brewster decided to make things a little more permanent for himself. So he took down his little blue tent and built a cabin at the same location. He still lives there.

Every spring he plants garden peas and beans. Every day he rides his bicycle around the swamp. And every Thursday night he plays the triangle with Wild Turkey and the Loblollies at the Jolie Blonde Café.